Easy Classical Masterworks for Trumpet

Easy Classical Masterworks for Trumpet

Music of Bach, Beethoven, Brahms, Handel, Haydn, Mozart, Schubert, Tchaikovsky, Vivaldi and Wagner

Easy Classical Masterworks for Trumpet

ISBN-13:978-1499174861
ISBN-10:1499174861

J.S. BACH

Bourrée, BWV 996

Johann Sebastian Bach

Moderato

Gavotte II, BWV 808

Johann Sebastian Bach

Andante

Menuett, BWV Anh 114

Johann Sebastian Bach

LUDWIG VAN BEETHOVEN

Chorfantasie, Op. 80

Ludwig van Beethoven

Für Elise, WoO 59

Ludwig van Beethoven

Allegro

Ode an die Freude, Op. 125

Ludwig van Beethoven

JOHANNES BRAHMS

Ungarischen Tänze Nº 5, WoO 1

Johannes Brahms

3. Sinfonie F-Dur, op. 90

Johannes Brahms

Poco allegretto

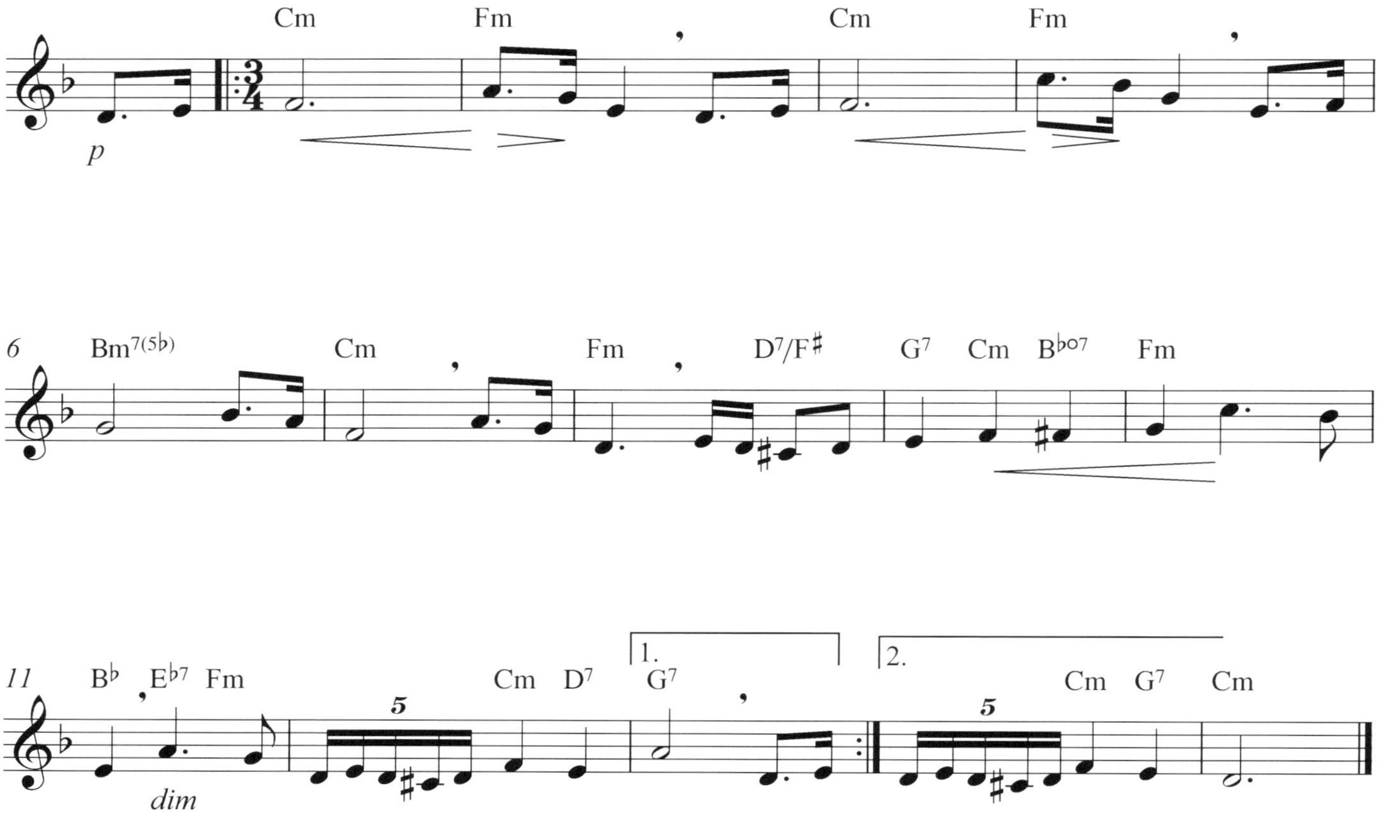

Guten Abend, gut' Nacht

Johannes Brahms

Adagio

GEORGE HAENDEL

Sarabande, HWV 437

George Frideric Handel

Hallelujah, HWV 56

George Frideric Handel

Water Music, HWV 349

George Frideric Handel

JOSEPH HAYON

Sinfonie Nr. 94 G-Dur, Hob.I:94

"mit dem Paukenschlag"

Joseph Haydn

WOLFANG AMADEUS MOZART

Ah vous dirais-je, Maman

Wolfgang Amadeus Mozart

Rondo Alla Turca, K. 331

Wolfgang Amadeus Mozart

Allegro

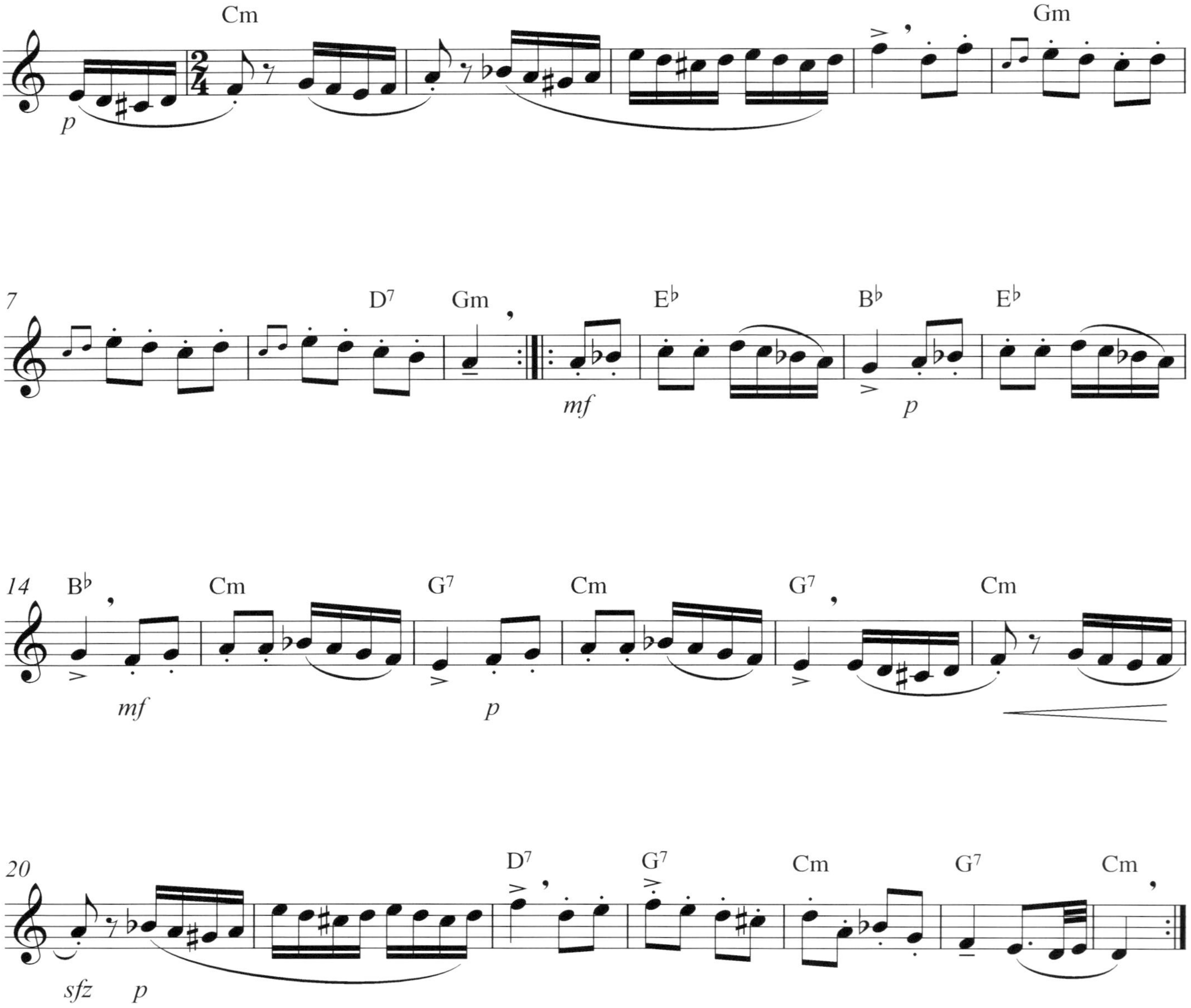

40. Sinfonie, K.550

Wolfgang Amadeus Mozart

Allegro molto

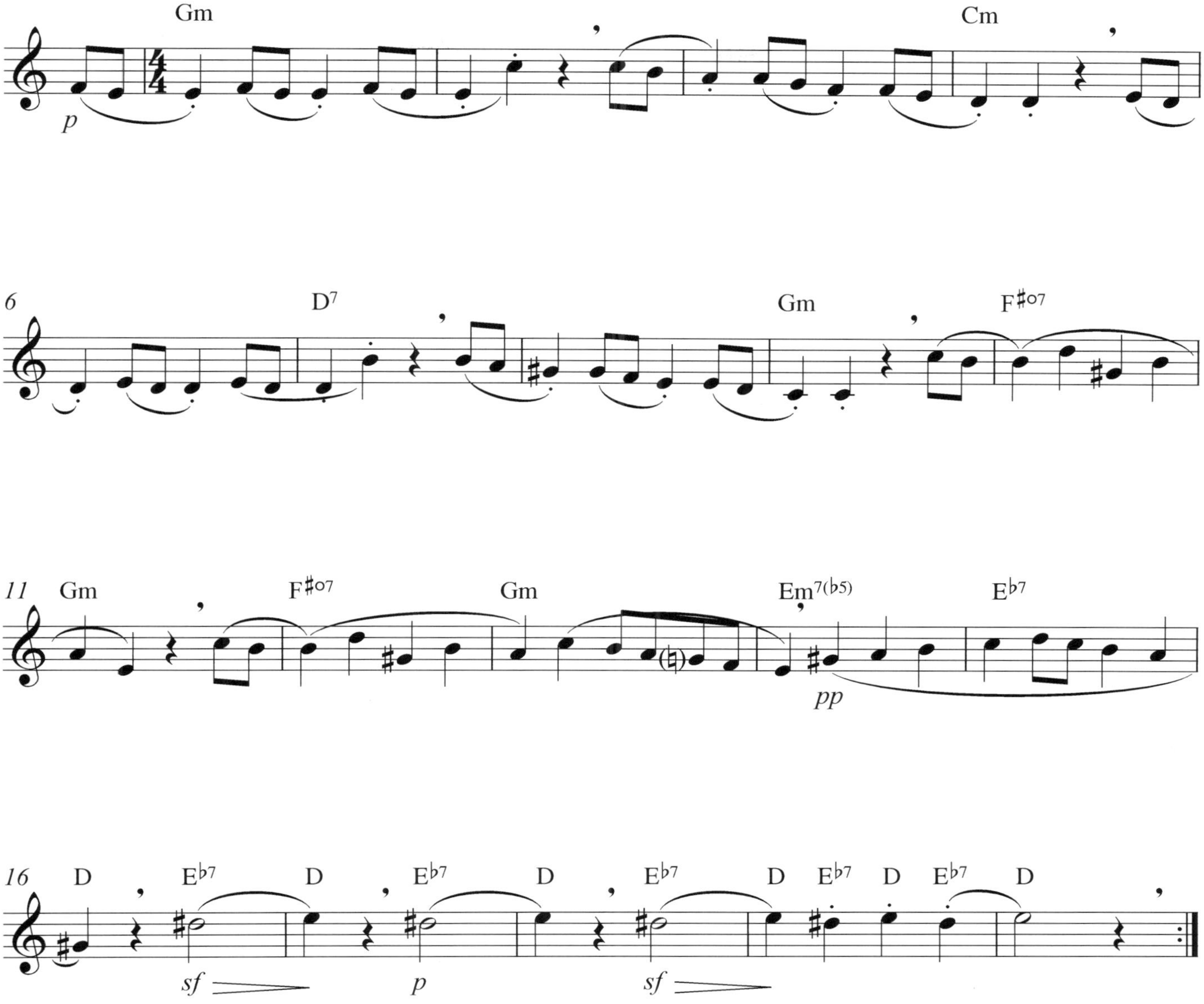

FRANZ SCHUBERT

Ständchen, D.957

Franz Schubert

PIOTR TCHAIKOWSKY

Щелкунчик, Op. 71a

(Dance of the Sugar Plum Fairy)

Piotr Ilyich Tchaikovsky

Andante ma non troppo

Щелкунчик, Ор. 71a

(March of The Nutcracker)

Piotr Ilyich Tchaikovsky

Tempo di marcia

Спящая красавица, Op.66a

(Sleeping Beauty Waltz)

Piotr Ilyich Tchaikovsky

ANTONIO VIVALDI

la Primavera, RV. 269

Antonio Vivaldi

Moderato

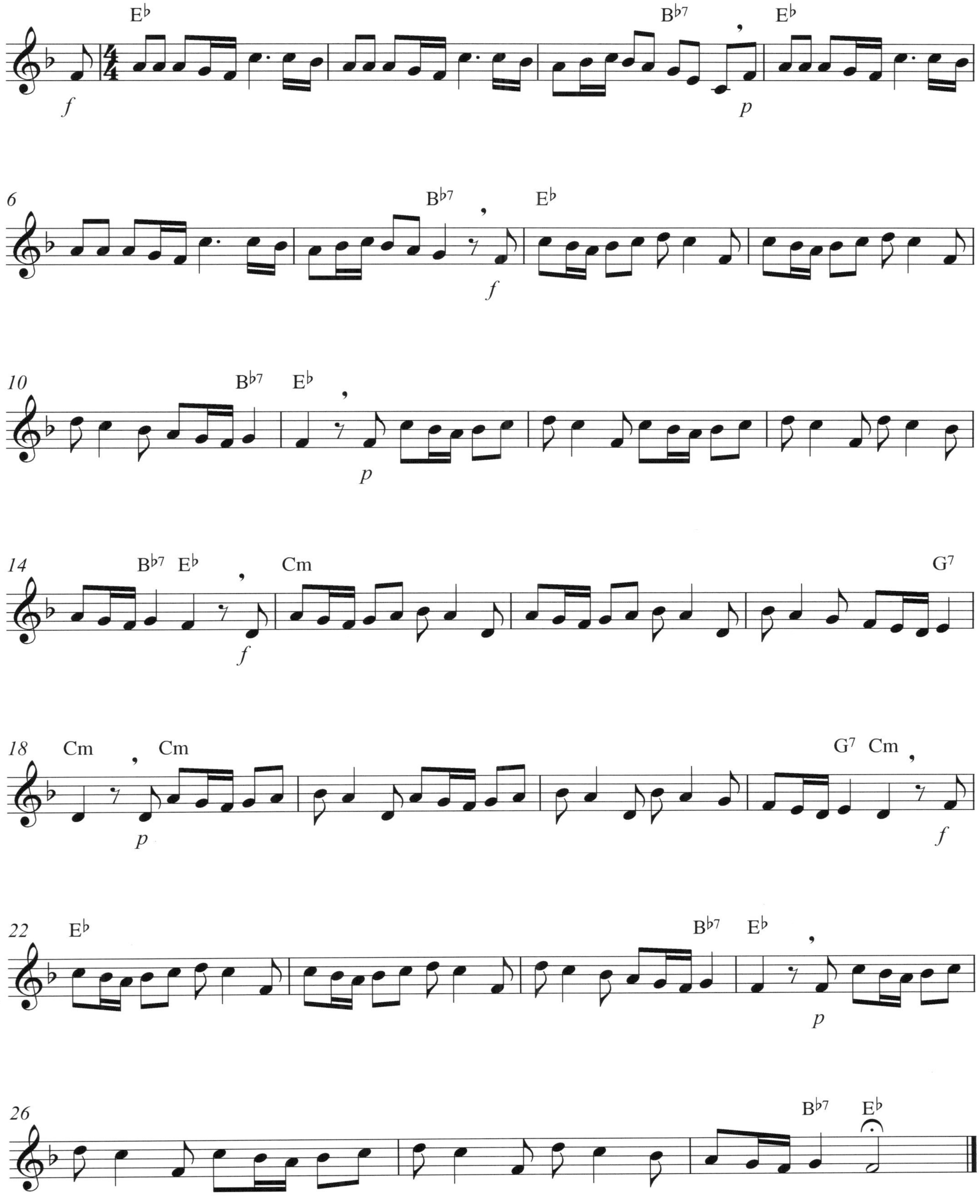

l'Estate, RV. 315

Antonio Vivaldi

Allegro non molto

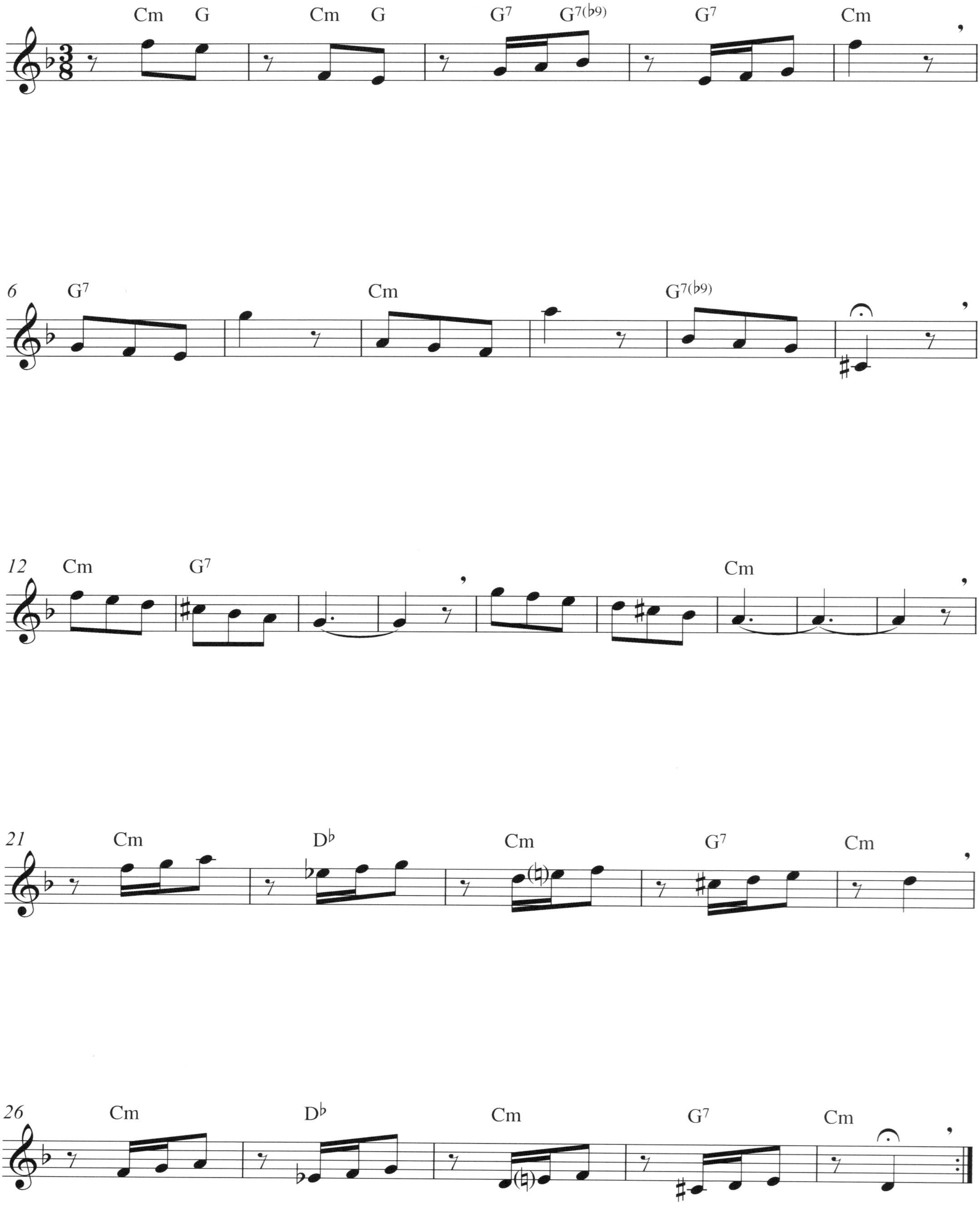

l'Autunno, RV. 293

Antonio Vivaldi

l'Inverno, RV. 297

Antonio Vivaldi

Largo

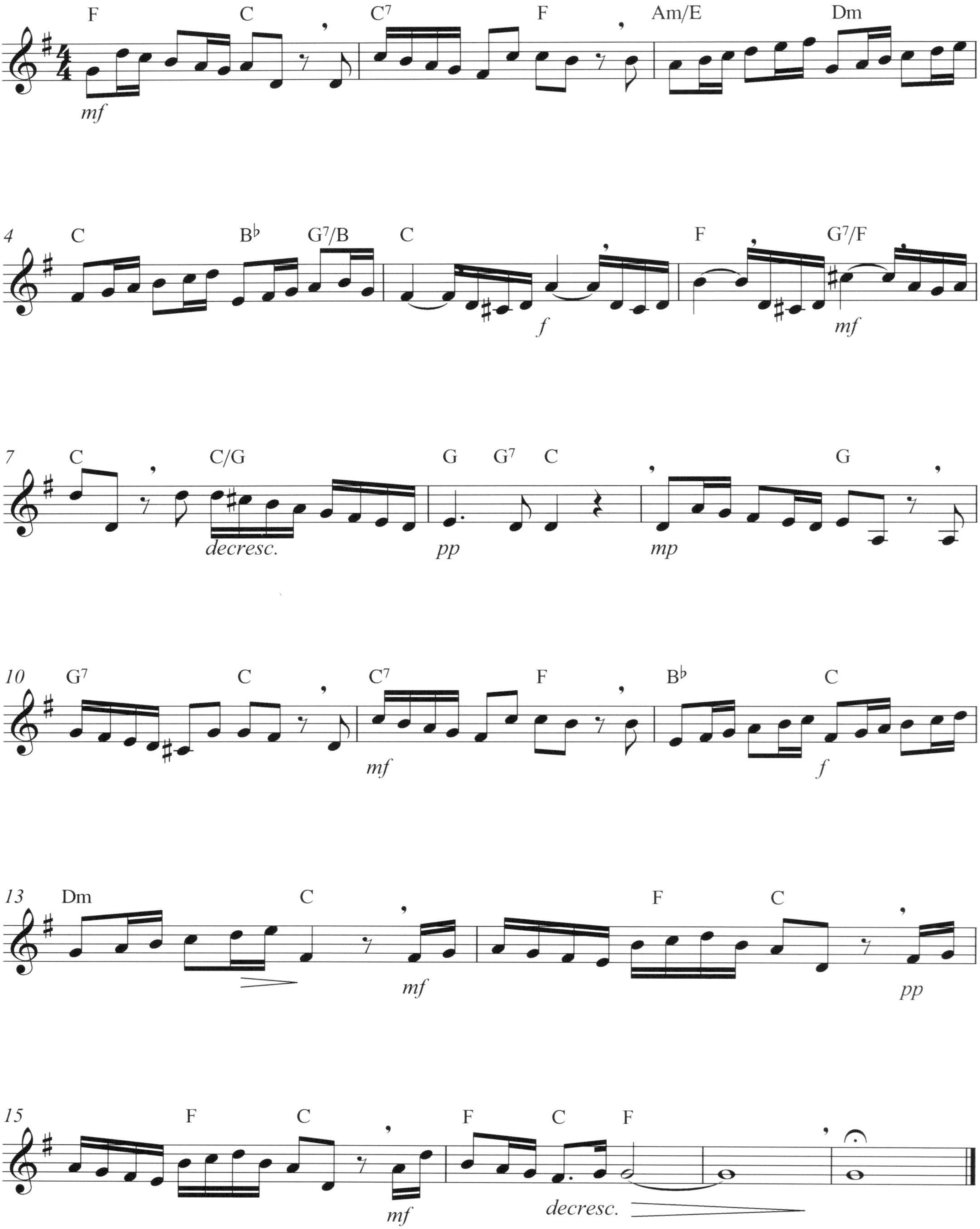

RICHARD WAGNER

Tannhäuser Ouvertüre, WWV 70

Richard Wagner

Made in the USA
San Bernardino, CA
19 July 2017